MR FIX-IT

A SHORT STORY

ALEXANDRIA BLAELOCK

Also by Alexandria Blaelock

SHORT STORY COLLECTIONS
The Histories of Hayward Hall
Lovelorn, Lovestruck and Love at First Sight
Common or Garden Variety Heroes
Case Files of the Wilkinson Detective Agency
Unavoidable Fates
Christmas Travesties
Five Faces of Felicia Clarke
Little Place Called Home
Security Directorate Dossiers v. 1.
Security Directorate Dossiers v. 2.

FICTION
That Love Nonsense
Taipan vs Brown
The Ghost and Ms Cox
Friends Like That
Weaving the Wildwood
Wolf vs Orb

MS BLAELOCK'S BOOKS
Stress Free Dinner Parties
Signature Wardrobe Planning
Holistic Personal Finance
Minimally Viable Housekeeping
Planning a Life Worth Living

PICTURE BOOKS
Australia Felix

A SELECTION OF AVAILABLE SHORT STORIES

Alma's Grace	Mince Pie Mystery
Blood and Bloody Profanity	Remains of Christmas
Cancelled by the Cartel	Shining Star
Dingo Hunting	Susan and the Gangster
Dream House	The Day the Schedule Broke
Honoris Virilis Respectu	The Trembling Tower

MR FIX-IT

A SHORT STORY

ALEXANDRIA BLAELOCK

BlueMere Books

MELBOURNE, AUSTRALIA

For permission requests, please contact enquiries@bluemerebooks.com.

Ordering Information:
Discounts are available on quantity purchases. For details, contact orders@bluemerebooks.com.

Mr Fix-it/Alexandria Blaelock
paperback ISBN: 978-1-923083-26-4
digital ISBN: 978-1-923083-27-1

Book Layout © BookDesignTemplates.com
Cover Art © Thanapol sinsrang/depositphotos

MR FIX-IT

Melissa got out of bed, and stretching mightily, walked across the wooden floor to her kitchen.

She'd endured a restless, but not quite sleepless night; the last few days had been too quiet, and she was feeling antsy, waiting for something to go wrong.

The kitchen was her favourite part of the studio apartment. Someone had painted the rough brick walls a cheerful yellow. The bright, creamy yellow of full fat, grass-fed cow's milk butter.

Delicious on hot, crisp sourdough toast with bitter orange marmalade.

Her one true luxury.

The wall was the first thing she saw when she opened the door to her apartment, and it never failed to make her smile. When she saw it, she could almost, but not quite, smell the cheerful scent of hot buttered toast (with said bitter orange marmalade).

Which was a wonderful gift because overall, her apartment was dark and dingy, with an excellent view of the wall of the apartment building next door.

The one that blocked the sun, and most of the fresh air.

That was so close she could touch it. Or could if the window she was looking through actually opened.

You had to ask, what was the point?

And after a bad night's sleep, what she *really* needed was a very strong cup of coffee.

Which was a shame, because it seemed she was all out of coffee. No beans, no grinds, no backup instant.

No coffee whatsoever.

Not even the smell of a used filter in the rubbish bin.

Melissa knew she'd brought some home the day before, so she checked her empty shopping bag store.

And then she realised.

It was a Day of Emptiness.

You know the kind.

The kind when you get out of bed to find there's no coffee.

And the toaster's on the fritz.

And the dog really *did* eat your homework.

Doesn't matter what you need, you've run out.

Because it's a Day of Emptiness, and everything important is empty.

Which is a great shame when you run a Mr Fix-it franchise, because you know it's going to be a busy day of Emptiness Emergencies, but all your Fix-it gear has disappeared from its appointed places because it just does on a Day of Emptiness.

And no one knows where it all goes, because you *never* hear about a Day of Fullness. A day where someone wakes up to find their house chock full of coffee that wasn't there the night before.

Wouldn't that be the most wonderful thing? You'd have to go buy a lottery ticket after that, wouldn't you?

Well, always assuming you liked coffee and weren't cursing the Gremlins because you preferred tea.

Or hot chocolate.

Melissa really hoped that actually happened, that the Emptiness Gremlins, as she called them, were more like little Robin Hoods and less like greedy and selfish creatures who couldn't get enough coffee.

They'd stolen her first set of tools from her red Mr Fix-it van. She knew it was them because there were no signs of a break-in and the CD player and her loose change were where she'd left them.

Since then she brought her most useful and valuable tools into the apartment with her but never left them in the same place twice. It'd worked so far, but she wasn't sure how long she'd get away with it.

The Emptiness Gremlins were prankish and just when you thought you were safe, you discovered they'd played you.

Sometimes she forgot where she'd hidden the tools and was terrified the Gremlins had found them after all.

Though it's possible (but not likely), they'd moved the tools instead of stealing them.

Little buggers.

But while they were frustrating and annoying, she was fonder of them than she'd admit (as if anyone would ask). She was pleased, and a little flattered, they thought she was worth their time when most humans didn't.

Did Gremlins have a concept of time?

She could make a fortune if she could somehow make a deal with them - they could mess up someone else's place, and she could go fix it.

Though that wasn't strictly speaking ethical.

Her job was to fix problems, not create them.

That being the case, she took a lightning-fast cold shower (hoping the hot water would be working when she got back), dressed in her cheery red franchise branded overalls and collected her hidden tool kit (which seemed intact) and left the apartment.

While she waited for her coffee,(warm, milky latte, no sugar thank you), she pulled out her tablet, and started checking the job feed; blown fuse (schedule), broken washing machine (schedule), lost memory (skip), spilt milk (schedule), banking error (skip), missing cat (skip), mangled key (schedule).

Wait, back up a minute, lost memory?

How intriguing.

Melissa couldn't think of a way to calculate how much time she'd need for that (or a price).

Assuming she took the job, which, as a technicality, should come after the easily schedulable stuff.

But the idea of fixing a lost memory was so captivating she had to scroll back and take the job before anyone else got to it. And she had to put it first on her list, regardless of the consequences.

She hoped the Emptiness Gremlins had been content with the coffee and the water heater and left her bank account intact.

And then, she felt obliged to release all the other jobs she'd booked to free up her time. She reassured herself that jobs came in a constant stream, night and day, and there would be something to charge for later.

Weirdly, the memory job was just a couple of doors down, so she left the van where she'd parked it the night before, and walked.

Despite her semi-sleepless night and the theft of her coffee, the latte and a stroll in the warm morning sunlight left her feeling rejuvenated, and ready for anything.

As she walked, tool bag swinging from one shoulder, she started formulating theories and preparing for what she might find when she arrived.

Like, would this person even remember they'd booked a Fix-it call?

But before she'd even made the most nebulous of attack plans, she was there, almost, but not quite ready to fly by the seat of her pants.

She knocked on the door.

"Who is it?" a baritone voice asked.

"Mr Fix-it," she replied.

"How can you be Mr Fix-it when you're not a Mr?"

"Uh, sir? It's a franchise."

"But I need Mr Fix-it. If I wanted Miss Fix-it, I would've called Miss Fix-it."

Melissa sighed, dropped her tool bag on the floor and massaged her temples.

Clearly lost memory included lost politeness.

"Sir? Do you want help with your lost memory or not?"

"I'm not sure I want it from you, Miss so-called Fix-it."

She thought of all those quick and easy jobs she'd just released back into the queue. She didn't need this aggravation on this of all mornings.

"That's fine sir. I'll just release your order back to the queue, and you can wait to see if a man will think your lost memory is worth his time.

"I just need your thumbprint to agree the release. If you'd just open the door, we can end this quickly."

She heard rattling as the man on the other side of the door set the security chain and opened the door a crack. A bright blue eye, half-hidden under a dark lock of hair, attempted to pin her with its gaze, but she wasn't having any of it.

She tapped a few buttons on her tablet's touch screen display and held it up to the door.

"There's a $50 call-out fee regardless of whether we go ahead with the job or not. Just tap the big red cancel button, and your account will be debited."

"I don't see why I should pay you anything. You're not Mr Fix-It."

"Sir, Mr Fix-It is too busy to see you, and he asked me to come instead. Are you going to disrespect him by refusing to pay the call-out fee?"

"Mr Fix-it sent you? Well, why didn't you just say so?"

She heard scrabbling as he released the security chain and opened the door.

She sighed, taking this job was probably the worst decision she'd ever made.

Honestly, you try to help people out, and all you get is grief.

She picked up her tool bag and walked into the biggest apartment she'd ever seen. Bright with sunshine streaming through the enormous plate-glass windows.

Glaring off the stark white painted walls.

Except for one, which was a gigantic painting of goodness knows what; all wildly uncomfortable swirls of colour and nothingness.

Or maybe it was emptiness?

Yes.

Emptiness.

It was like a black hole sucking in all the somethingness out of the apartment.

Maybe the world.

That would explain why the apartment didn't seem to have any furniture.

She looked up again at the painted wall, half expecting to see chair legs poking out of it.

No wonder this guy had lost his memory.

"Sir, can you tell me your name?"

"No."

"Can you tell me where your furniture went?"

"No.

"Well, not really. I'm not sure there was ever any furniture in here."

She tapped her tablet screen a few times and started to make notes, "what's the last thing you remember then?"

"I don't remember anything. I just woke up here."

"So, can you remember where you left your pants, Sir?"

"My pants? What do you mean my pants?"

Melissa gestured at the bare legs poking out from under his long button-down shirt. "Don't make me ask if you remember what pants are sir?"

He looked down at his legs and then back at hers.

And then he sort of strode around the empty room as if he might suddenly see a pile of clothing that wasn't there before.

"I don't understand," he said, "why don't I have any pants?

"Why do I have an empty space in my head where all this stuff should be?"

"That would be the Emptiness Gremlins Sir."

"Emptiness Gremlins? Are they a thing? Emptiness Gremlins?"

Melissa thought she saw something move out of the corner of her eye, but when she turned to look, there was nothing there.

"I couldn't say Sir, they're just how I explain missing things."

"Emptiness Gremlins. They feel real, what do they do?"

"They take things Sir, the important things."

"Like memories?"

"Well, I was thinking of more tangible things like coffee, your favourite pen and hair ribbons. But given little creatures that steal things probably aren't real, I expect they'd be able to take intangible things too."

"But why *all* my memories?"

"Were they important Sir?"

"To me or to them?"

"To you, I guess. They only ever take things that are important to me."

"But why take any memories, let alone all of them?"

Once again, Melissa thought something moved and turned to follow it, only this time she ended up back facing the painting wall.

Only it looked different somehow. Not enough that she could say definitively, but enough to startle her into dropping her half-drunk latte.

Which hit the painting instead of the floor, and as she watched, she could see it getting smaller as it fell further and further into the wall.

"Uh, Sir? Do you know how long this painting has been here?"

"Painting, what painting?" He turned to face her, silhouetted against the painted wall, "is that painting moving?"

"It is, and I'm not convinced it's a painting."

Melissa walked towards the corner of the room to see if she could find out how the image, for the want of a better word, worked.

The man caught her up in his arms, spinning her around so he was between her and the wall. "I don't think it's safe for you to get too close to the wall."

Melissa allowed herself to enjoy the warmth of his body for a moment before she took a deep breath and took a step back.

He smelled like fresh Seville orange juice.

She smiled, though she hadn't meant to. "I'm Mr Fix-It remember. I think if we can fix the image, we can fix your memory."

Something flickered again in the corner of her eye.

"Are you seeing those flickery things out of the corner of your eye too?"

He turned one way, and then the other. And then he did a sort of zig-zag and pointed a finger, "you mean those creatures?"

Where he was pointing, six little imp-like creatures were becoming apparent.

They looked a bit like axolotls standing upright. Sort of transparent pinky coloured, with darker pink manes, wings and tails.

It seemed to Melissa, as they shuffled their feet, they were embarrassed about being caught. And logically, if you were an invisible creature, it'd have to be a bit disconcerting.

"Are they Emptiness Gremlins do you think?" she asked.

"Off the top of my head I can't think what else they might be, can you?" He started lowering his finger, and one of them winked out.

"Wait!"

He stopped moving.

"You seem to be controlling them. Could you move your finger sideways for a sec?"

He frowned a little but did as she asked.

It was as if his finger was a spotlight, playing across the group, some showing up and some going "dark" as his finger moved.

He moved his finger back and forward across the group, "fascinating," he said.

"Do you know if you've seen them before?"

"Oh yes, they're always around."

"So, you can see invisible creatures no one else can," she reached into her bib pocket and pulled out a small wrapped chocolate.

"Really, you can't see them?"

"Only where your finger points them out."

She unwrapped the wrapper to find it empty, then realised one of the Gremlins was eating something.

Melissa could almost hear the others berating it. It definitely shrugged one shoulder at them.

"That Gremlin stole your chocolate," he said, "did you see how fast it moved?"

"No," she replied, tossing the wrapper at the painted wall and watching it disappear. "So you can see them, you can make others see them, and—"

"That's just rude, you apologise," he said.

She put her hands on her hips, "apologise for what?"

"Not you, Trax over there."

She looked again at the gremlins, and the surly one who stole her chocolate was talking back to lost memory guy.

He flicked a finger at it, and it disappeared into the painting.

There was a sort of collective intake of breath from the other gremlins, and they sort of smartened up.

One of them made a gesture to ward off bad luck and then cowered back as the guy leaned towards it.

"Right," said Melissa, "you can see them, and you can control them. It seems to me you're in a position of control. Do you think you could be their King?"

"How could I be their King if I don't look like them?"

"You don't remember anything; how do you know you don't look like them?"

"I don't know, I just know I look like you.

"Only different.

"But more like you than them."

"So if you're not their King, how do you control them?"

"I don't know.

"Why are you asking me all these questions?"

"Because you asked me to fix your lost memory."

"Oh yeah, right."

"Ok, try this then, what are their names?"

"Their names?"

"Yes, their names?"

"Names, right. Then there's Tukumi, Kyic, Ugher, Dox, Krebo and Dan."

"Dan?"

"Yes, Dan. That one over there."

The gremlin who made the warding gesture waved his hand backwards and forwards a few times, and Melissa couldn't help but smile.

"Dan, right, Hi!," she said waving at the creature.

"So is Dox related to Trax?"

"Oh yes, they're littermates."

"And how do you know that?"

"Because I was there when they were made. They were so cute when they were little."

"And how do you know that?"

"Because I'm always there when they're made."

"Ah, what's the delicate way to answer that question? Are you the breeder?"

"Don't be silly, I'm the boss."

"Isn't the "boss" the same thing as the King?"

"Well, I don't have a crown or anything."

Melissa eyed the headdress that was starting to materialise on top of his head. She pointed at it, "what's that then?"

He went to touch the top of his head and dislodged it.

She went to grab it in case it fell into the painting as well, but it hit the floor.

As she bent to pick it up, and again he wrapped her in his arms and placed himself between her and the crown, "you can't touch it."

"Why not?"

"Because you are not the King." He pulled a smaller one out of the air, "you should take this one."

"Why?"

"Because it's the Queen's," he put it on her head, "it belongs to you, just like the Emptiness Gremlins do."

She looked at the creatures again, and she found she could see them clearly.

They were doing a victory dance.

And she looked at the wall, and it seemed like the painting was unwinding, undoing all the emptiness it had created.

She ducked as Trax came rocketing out of the picture.

She didn't know how long she'd have to wait for her memory to come back, but she was pretty sure it would be worth the wait.

THE END

As a small token of my thanks for reading...

Please enjoy one time 10% off everything
(excluding shipping)

at alexandriablaelock.com

with the code trax10.

Turn the page for some ideas where to use it,

Please consider The Ghost and Ms Cox

Life interrupted

To say the letter was a surprise was an understatement. It arrived addressed to Miss Finlay Cox, which made the contents even more extraordinary.

Orphan Finn Cox inherits a cottage. Thinks it holds the key to her origins. Of course she takes a look. Who wouldn't?

But when she gets there, she gets more than she bargained for.

Is it friend, family or foe?

Weaving the Wildwood

All she wants is a place of her own.

When Alison Porter finds a tiny cottage for sale, she thinks her dreams have come true. Inside virgin bushland, "Crow Cottage" sits on the smallest parcel of cleared land.

It's old. It's run down. It's keeping a secret.

Stumbling through a mysterious portal in the garden, she finds herself in a place of mystery and intrigue. As the past, present and future collide, she must unravel the secret, for only then can she reweave the tapestry of time.

If you love a story of twists and turns, where nothing is what it seems, grab Weaving the Wildwood today.

The Histories of Hayward Hall

Meet Morag Clementine. The new housekeeper at historic Hayward Hall.

Her practical and capable attitude usually keeps her out of trouble.

bove all, her no-nonsense, get it done approach. And her get in the middle of the scrum outlook. Just as well, because Hayward Hall needs someone like her.

In this genre-spanning collection of original stories, Morag finds herself ensnared in the History of Hayward Hall...

No ordinary housekeeper, can Morag save the house, one century at a time?

Little Place Called Home

Home is where the heart is

You can struggle to find the place you call home. It's not a place, it's a feeling.

You'll know it when you find it.

This collection of short stories explores our search for a place we can call home.

Short, sweet and relatable, these stories will make you homesick for places you've never been.

Perhaps you'll carry your new books in one of these bags

*And enjoy them while you're drinking
from one of these mugs*

www.ingramcontent.com/pod-product-compliance
Lightning Source LLC
Chambersburg PA
CBHW051829180726
48283CB00004BA/1371